Engineer Ari
and the
Sukkah Express

by Deborah Bodin Cohen
Illustrations by Shahar Kober

KAR-BEN
PUBLISHING

For Jesse Benjamin—a story of friendship for
my beloved son who makes friends wherever he goes—D.B.C.

Text copyright © 2010 by Deborah Bodin Cohen
Illustrations © 2010 Lerner Publishing Group, Inc.
Photo p.32 by Garabad Krikorian, Armenian Patriarchate Collection

KAR-BEN PUBLISHING
A division of Lerner Publishing Group, Inc.
241 First Avenue North
Minneapolis, MN 55401 U.S.A.
1-800-4KARBEN

Website address: www.karben.com

Library of Congress Cataloging-in-Publication Data

Cohen, Deborah Bodin, 1968–
    Engineer Ari and the sukkah express / by Deborah Bodin Cohen ; illustrated by Shahar Kober.
       p.   cm.
    Summary: When the friends he has made on the new railroad line give Engineer Ari things to help build and decorate a sukkah in his courtyard, he is sad that they cannot come and enjoy it with him.
    ISBN 978-0-7613-5126-9 (lib. bdg. : alk. paper)
    [1. Sukkah--Fiction. 2. Sukkot--Fiction. 3. Jews--Fiction. 4. Railroad trains--Fiction.] I. Kober, Shahar, ill. II. Title.
    PZ7.C6623Eng 2010
    [E—dc22   2009001876

Manufactured in the United States of America
1 – VI – 7/15/10

GLOSSARY

Etrog: lemon-like fruit

Lulav: palm branch bound with sprigs of myrtle and willow

Sukkot: harvest holiday

Sukkah: temporary booth built to celebrate Sukkot

Todah Rabah: thank you (Hebrew)

Yom Kippur: Day of Atonement

"Boker tov, good morning," Engineer Ari called to his friend Jessie. "It's time to build our sukkah."

Engineer Ari breathed in the crisp autumn air. It was the morning after Yom Kippur.

"Good morning to you," answered Jessie, coming out of the house. "But where is Nathaniel? He is so handy with a saw and hammer. We need his help."

Just then, Nathaniel arrived, carrying his tool box. "I'm ready!" he said. "Let's go down to the railway station. When the workers finished the tracks, they left behind some wood that will be perfect for our sukkah."

At the station, the three engineers sorted through the woodpile and carried pieces of lumber back to Ari's courtyard.

Ari steadied the ladder, while Jessie held the boards for Nathaniel to nail together. As the frame took shape, the three friends stood back to admire their handiwork.

"Now we need branches for the roof and fruit for decorations," said Jessie.

"And a lulav and etrog to shake in the sukkah," added Nathaniel.

"Don't worry," answered Ari. "I'm driving the train to Jerusalem tomorrow, and I have an idea."

The next morning, Engineer Ari CHUG-A-LUGGED out of Jaffa Station. Since the railway opened, he had made many new friends along his route. He stopped his engine in an olive grove. His new friend Hadas was tending the trees.

"Do you have branches that I could use for the roof of my sukkah?" he asked her.

"Plenty!" answered Hadas. "Take as many as you need. Remember, a sukkah's roof needs to be thick enough to keep out the rain . . ."

". . . but thin enough to see the stars," finished Engineer Ari with a wink. "Thank you, Hadas. Todah rabah."

The crowd climbed onto the train, carrying lulavs and etrogs. Children hung fruit from the sukkah's roof.

Engineer Ari tugged the whistle cord, "Toot, toot." He pulled back the throttle and the Sukkah Express CHUG-a-LUGGED out of the station. It was time to celebrate with friends, new and old.

⚞⟋⟍ Author's Note ⟍⟋⚟

On August 27, 1892, the first train steamed into Jerusalem from Jaffa, carrying passengers and cargo. A month later, during the High Holidays, the railway officially opened. The train shortened the trip between the Mediterranean coast and Jerusalem from 3 days to 3½ hours. Eliezer Ben-Yehuda, the father of modern Hebrew, who lived in Jerusalem at the time, coined the word *rakevet* (train) from the Biblical word for "chariot."

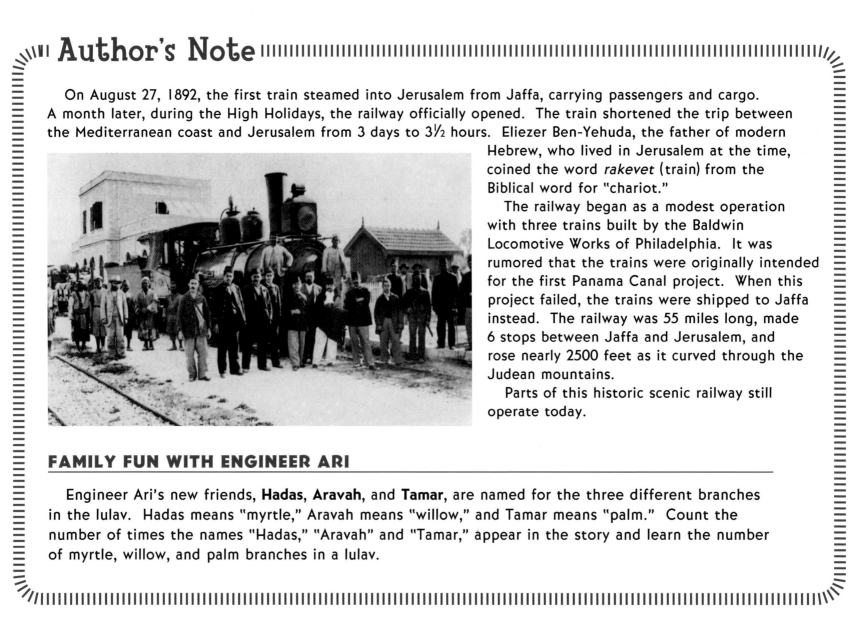

The railway began as a modest operation with three trains built by the Baldwin Locomotive Works of Philadelphia. It was rumored that the trains were originally intended for the first Panama Canal project. When this project failed, the trains were shipped to Jaffa instead. The railway was 55 miles long, made 6 stops between Jaffa and Jerusalem, and rose nearly 2500 feet as it curved through the Judean mountains.

Parts of this historic scenic railway still operate today.

FAMILY FUN WITH ENGINEER ARI

Engineer Ari's new friends, **Hadas**, **Aravah**, and **Tamar**, are named for the three different branches in the lulav. Hadas means "myrtle," Aravah means "willow," and Tamar means "palm." Count the number of times the names "Hadas," "Aravah" and "Tamar," appear in the story and learn the number of myrtle, willow, and palm branches in a lulav.